The Friendly C[illegible] Moon City

Book 4: The Underground City

Mark Mulle

DEDICATION

This book is dedicated to all Minecraft lovers.

CONTENTS

DAY 1

I had been happily minding my own business when David had to come over and ruin it.

Okay, maybe that sounds a bit harsh. But trust me – I have known David long enough now to know that when he runs over at full speed to my house, it is only going to lead to trouble for me.

Don't believe me? Alright. After we saved the Over World from Lucas, the creeper king who wanted to drag everyone into the Nether so he could rule them, things settled down. Everyone was able to work with our village and David's village. Slowly, people came to understand that even though we were creepers, we weren't the typical creepers that they dealt with. We weren't going to explode on sight or attack them.

But David didn't want to sit around and remain in the village. Even though his aunt, Margery, wanted nothing more than for him to focus at things at home, David had spent hours combing through old stories and legends. He said if Lucas was true, who knew what else was out there?

He had run over here a few times, each time claiming he knew of where to find some sort of treasure. There was the time he dragged me to the beach to find some sort of cave where there would be wither skeletons made out of gold. There weren't. There was another time where we went to Sun City nearby because he had read a story about how there was apparently a secret society there filled with gold and jewels. There wasn't.

So when David burst into my house today, and would be talking about some new treasure that he had discovered, I wasn't interested.

"Mike, you busy?" He said to me as he came into my house without knocking.

"Almost always, yeah." I replied as I shoved another book in the bookshelf.

Since we had saved the Over World, I had tried to keep things pretty quiet. I helped out around our village and would sometimes take goods and other items to David's village. Beth stepped down as mayor and offered me the position but I said no. I was determined to live quietly from now on. No more adventures for me. I had enough of that.

"Busy what, putting books away?" David joked.

"Hey, these are rare books. I'm trying to organize them because I'm going to try to open up a library here."

David pulled one of the books off the shelf and looked at it, "This is really old. Where did you find these?"

"Mostly through trading."

Collecting the books had been a nice way to pass the time. It was interesting and more importantly – it was safe. There weren't going to be any wither skeletons jumping out at me over some dusty old books.

"A library, huh?" David asked me as he flipped the book open.

"That's right. Then everyone can study these old books and read about the Over World," I looked over at him, "What brought you over here in such a hurry?"

"Margery. She wanted to invite you over for dinner."

"So you hurried over here for a dinner invite?"

"Nah, I was supposed to come by yesterday and tell you but I forgot." David admitted as he looked through a pile of books I had on the floor.

I hadn't seen Margery in a while. Going over to her place for dinner sounded like a nice time. I was also relieved that David had hurried over here for a dinner invite and not some sort of crazy adventure.

"Sure. Do we leave now? Let me get my things."

"Yeah, take your time." David replied, looking at one of the other books.

I went to the other room to grab my things. Even though there was a safe trail to get to David's village now, I still liked to be prepared. It only took me a minute or so to get ready. When I came back into the main room, David had a strange look on his face. Something looked off but I couldn't pinpoint it.

"You okay?" I asked him.

"Yeah, I'm great. Come on, let's go."

I followed David out the front door. My village sprawled out in front of me. We had grown recently, having been able to rebuild the damage that happened when the Nether creatures were attacking us. Between that and the fact we did trade with the rest of the Over World now, we were doing really well for ourselves.

My friend, Alex, lived next door to me. He had taken up gardening even though creepers gardening weren't exactly common. The sight of him trying to garden was always amusing. Currently he was struggling with a shovel, trying to dig up a space in the back of his garden.

"Doing alright, Alex?" David called out to him.

Alex looked up and waved, "I'll figure it out!"

"Gotta admire his determination." David mumbled to me as we walked by.

"Sure, that's one way of wording it." I replied.

He laughed and we started to catch up on what had been going on as we cut across the village. Along the way, people stopped to wave at us or say hi.

"Forgot how popular we are here," David said as we neared the pathway, "You used to it yet?"

"No. Still feels sort of weird."

"I still think you should have agreed to be mayor."

I shook my head, "I wasn't ready for that. Too much to do. After what we went through, I just want to live quietly."

That strange look crossed David's face and then he smiled, "Yeah, of course. Come on. We better walk quickly so we aren't late."

As I watched David leave, I didn't know why but I just knew that there was something else going on in that head of his.

DAY 2

Margery was happy to see me. She was in charge of this village and had been extremely helpful when I had been in trouble before. She hurried me to my seat and went to get the food.

"I told David to tell you yesterday but he had his head in the clouds as usual." She was saying to me.

David was outside, having stopped to talk to someone who wanted to haggle with him for some new equipment. I could see him outside the window.

"How is he doing, anyway?" I asked her, "He seems…different."

"Ever since you two stopped Lucas down there in the Nether, he's convinced that there is more to the world out there than what we can see. He's always reading old books or studying old stories to find more legends. Well – you know that. He's dragged you on a couple."

She put down a plate of food in front of me as I replied, "Yeah, and nothing had come out of those trips. I figured he would have known that by now."

Margery sighed, "No, not yet. He's still sure that there is something else out there. That all the legends are true. Something like that."

David came just then and the conversation stopped. As we all began to eat and catch up, I couldn't help but wonder what my friend was up to. Did he really think there was more to the world than what we could see?

I know that Lucas had been a legend but he had been real. He really had been trying to get creepers down there to reclaim his throne. Was that enough to convince David there were all sorts of strange things going on?

Dinner went well. Nothing strange was brought up. We caught up on what was going on with our villages. When we finished, I helped clean up. We had spoken a little too long and now the moon was high up in the sky.

"You should stay here tonight, Mike," Margery said to me, "It's already dark outside and I wouldn't want you to run into anything dangerous."

"Sounds good. I'll take the guest room." I said through a yawn.

So here I am, curled up in bed in the guest room. I don't mind staying here sometimes. It is nice to get out of my home village. Even though I don't have any sort of taste for adventure, everything we went through allowed for me to see there is an entire world out there. I wouldn't want to spend every day back home.

I still can't help but feel as if something is going on with David. It is past midnight by now and I should be asleep. But I keep seeing that expression on his face when I had come back into the room. It was as if he had discovered something. But what?

I should go to sleep. No use in trying to stay up and figure David out.

DAY 3

I woke up to someone shaking me.

I blinked and realized it was David hovering over me. I propped myself up.

"What are you doing?" I asked, confused and looking out the window, "It's still night. What time is it?"

"Like three in the morning."

"And you're waking me up because?"

David sat down at the edge of the bed. He was holding something in his lap. My eyes were still blurry from sleep.

"I found something," David said to me as I did so, "In this book."

I lowered my hands and blinked, "That's my book!"

It was the book that he had been looking at yesterday. He must have taken it when I had stepped into the other room to get my things. That was why he had had that funny look on his face when I had come back.

"Well, technically, yes, but you said it yourself that you were making a library. I just borrowed it early."

"David, this still doesn't explain why you are waking me up this late."

"Early. I mean, once again…it's technically morning."

"If you say the word 'technically' one more time…"

David held up his hands and went, "Alright, alright. Listen, I've been looking for this book. I've been looking for it everywhere, actually."

"Why?"

He flipped it open. It was an incredibly old book and smelled musty. Since it had been in a pile of books I hadn't gotten to yet, I hadn't looked in it at all. The insides were full of drawings. None of them made sense to me. But they apparently made sense to David because he went to a certain page and pointed.

"See?" He said triumphantly.

I looked over his shoulder. The drawing showed a city. Underneath the city there was a drawing of another city. It didn't mean anything to me and I shrugged.

"Come on," David said impatiently, "You don't recognize that city?"

"No. It is three in the morning. I'm tired. You woke me up because you like a drawing in one of my books."

He was shaking his head, "No, come on! That's Sun City!"

I looked at the drawing closer but it didn't look like Sun City to me. Sun City was home of the king. It was also where we had gone when David had been convinced there had been that secret society living there.

I groaned, "Is this about that society and the jewels or whatever?"

"No, look. The Sun City is up here. And this is the Moon City. Look, they're even marked."

He pointed to a small sun drawn on the top half of the drawing. Then he flipped the book over and pointed to a moon symbol on the bottom. I was too tired to make any sense of this and merely shrugged.

David kept going, "There is a legend that the Moon City is underneath the Sun City. Originally, I had dismissed it as false. That's why I was chasing after that secret society rumor."

"Which was, in fact, nothing."

"Right. Dead end, anyway. But this – this book is filled with clues and proof that the Moon City is directly underneath the Sun City."

"And so?" I said, trying to lose my patience, "David, I know going to the Nether and seeing Lucas and saving people – I know you miss that sort of action and adventure but…it's done with. Chasing after these old legends is a waste of time."

"How can you say that? We saw one of the legends were true with our own eyes! I know I've had dead ends since then but this Moon City…this might be the real deal."

"So, what else does this book say? Does it tell us how to get into it? Does it explain why there would even be a city underneath the Sun City? Would the king know? Does it even matter?"

"I have a theory that the king is part of the secret society that is protecting –"

I groaned, "David, come on. Come on! Do you hear yourself? You're chasing after nothing. Seriously. You're being silly. These are just stories. So, we got lucky with Lucas being real. But something like this – I mean, do you hear yourself?"

David talked over me, "That the king is part of a secret society bound to protect the Moon City! That it is underneath the Sun City and is brimming with treasure. Real treasure. Items we haven't even seen in the Over World before. Armor made not only of diamonds but of other jewels, blended and welded together to make something new. Books about what the world was like before we were here. All sorts of things in the Moon City!"

"And what? You want to go to the Sun City and talk to the king? Be like 'hey, are you part of a secret society hiding another city underneath this one?' and he'll be like 'ah, I am. Here is the key'. Is that what you think will happen?"

"I'm going, Mike. You can come with me or you can stay behind, collecting books, refusing to be mayor, refusing to go to the Sun City, refusing to do anything because even though we saw all that crazy stuff, you don't want to go seek out anything new. Where was that guy who signed up for the chance to leave the village?"

I wanted to tell him 'that guy' had only signed up because everyone else around him had and he didn't want to look foolish. I wanted to tell him that I wanted a quiet life now even if it was boring.

But I was too angry at the time to say that and instead I said, "You're being foolish. Margery wants you to be mayor one day. But you won't be if you keep running off for things that don't exist."

David stood up after I said this and stared down at me. His lips were in a thin line. He was angry, I realized, as he stared hard at me.

"I thought, deep down, Mike, you were bored too. I really thought you'd want to check this out with me. But I guess I was wrong. So I'll do it myself. I'm leaving in three days."

He stormed out, leaving me alone in the room. I didn't see him the next morning and I walked back to the village alone.Even though I tried to put our fight out of my mind, it was impossible to.

Was David right? Was I just content to stay back home because I didn't want to deal with anything else? Maybe I really did want to stick my head in the sand and pretend there weren't things out there. We had seen with our own eyes Lucas as the Creeper King down in the Nether. People would even say a village full of friendly creepers was a legend but here we were.

Maybe it doesn't matter if I truly believe if it is real or not. David is going to the Sun City again to try to find this silly, underground city. If he goes alone, he won't have anyone helping him or giving him back up. Since I can't talk him out of it, then maybe to be a good friend, I have to go anyway.

A lot to think about and I only have three days to decide.

DAY 4

I met up with David as he was leaving his aunt's house. He turned around and stopped when he saw me.

"Hey." I said, unsure if he would even want me to come along with him now.

He walked over to me. He had a backpack slung over one shoulder and his sword hitched to his waist. He looked me up and down.

"You brought your bow?" He said, pointing to the bow on my back.

"Ah, yeah. Been practicing with it. I'm pretty good now." I replied.

It was true. The bow had been specially made for me by Alex. It allowed me to work it with my multiple hands.

"Didn't know you still trained with weapons. Figured you put them away." David said, still clearly bothered by our fight.

"Figured it'd be good just in case something happened like the Nether portals opening."

"So, why are you here?"

"If you still want me to come with you, I want to come." I told him.

It was true. I had spent the last three days debating if I was going to go or not. But ultimately, I knew that I had to. David needed someone with him to keep him from running headfirst into danger. I didn't think there were any truths to the legends but did that matter? Let David believe it. I would just go because he was my friend.

He stared at me for a few seconds before nodding, "Yeah, sure. Come on. We're cutting through the jungle."

"Great. Love that place." I joked as we headed towards it.

David finally smiled at this, "Yeah, me too."

We were both remembering how we had run into each other there when regular creepers had exploded at us. We headed into the jungle once again.

Later that night

Honestly, I cannot stand this jungle. I'm pretty sure I wrote that down already last time I was here. But I really can't stand it.

First off, when David said we were cutting through, I assumed we would be out of the jungle in an hour. Maybe two. Apparently 'cutting through' to David means spending the entire day in the jungle.

He says it is the quickest way to the Sun City instead of going over one village and trying to get a ride there. Fine except the jungle is terrible to go through. Progress felt slow to me although David kept saying we were making good time.

Not good enough. We weren't going to make it to the Sun City by nightfall which meant we had to make camp in the jungle. Just what I wanted – to stay overnight in the jungle.

We had been trying to figure out where to make camp and I had been secretly wondering why in the world I had decided to show up after all when I heard the noise. It was a soft chittering noise I knew all too well.

David heard it too and unsheathed his sword. I grabbed my bow. Spiders were somewhere in the darkness. We had one torch set up but if there were a group of them, they could still grab at us if we left the safety of the light.

"Better to clear them out now." David said as I notched an arrow in my bow.

"Man, I don't like this place." I grumbled.

The chittering noises grew louder. It was a group of spiders by the amount of noise they were making. Then they burst through the darkness and lunged at us. I let my arrow go and it hit the first spider that had lunged at David. Then I notched another arrow.

Next to me, David was jumping into the fight. I could tell that he had been practicing with his sword and shield which didn't surprise me. Since he was so convinced there was so much to see in the world, of course he would be practicing.

We took two of the spiders down easily but three more were circling around us. One distracted me and another attacked from the back. I was thrown to the ground and got a mouth full of dirt.

"You okay?" David called over to me as I got to my feet.

"Wonderful!" I called back as I fired an arrow into the nearest spider.

The final two spiders seemed to be wondering if this had been a smart idea. They split up and one came after each of us. I fired an arrow but it missed and lodged into the tree behind the spider. I was knocked back to the ground with the spider on top of me.

"Mike!" David cried out at me.

I tried to keep the spider's teeth off of me. The spider was heavy and too strong to just push off of me. As I struggled, David was fending off the spider that was coming after him. He rolled by the spider and picked up the torch that we had shoved in the ground.

Then he threw it towards me. The spider saw the flames coming towards it and lurched backwards in fear. This gave me enough time to push it off of me. The spider was scampering away from the flame of the torch. I grabbed my bow and fired off another shot.

This time it landed and the spider turned to ash. Behind me, David finished off the spider that had been attacking him. Silence filled up the jungle.

"You okay?" David asked me.

"Yeah. Good idea with the flame though."

David helped me to my feet, "You have gotten a lot better with that bow."

"You too, with the sword."

He looked down at it, "Yeah, well. Figured I shouldn't let my skills get rusty."

I sighed, "Can we please set up camp now? All I want to do is sleep."

I managed to write in here to catch up everything that had happened but I am too tired to stay awake any longer. I am hoping tomorrow we will find the Sun City and I get to sleep in a real bed.

DAY 5

The Sun City was sprawled out in front of us by the middle of the afternoon. It looked the same since the last time we had been here. It had high walls to keep out any enemies but once you got past the walls, the city was like a glittering jewel. The homes were made out of the nicest materials. Stores sold and crafted anything someone could think of.

The Sun City was on a large hill. On the very top of the hill was the king. Even though all the villages had mayors to take care of the day to day affairs, the king still had the most control over the Over World. Any major choices were left up to him.

We had never met the king directly. It had almost happened. After we had taken care of Lucas, someone who spoke for the king came to see us. They had mentioned that we might get to meet the king but it never ended up happening. What the king did do, however, was let everyone know about our village. That meant that people knew there were friendly creepers out there. Sure, people still got a bit scared around us but at least I could walk around Sun City and not have anyone panic.

"Alright, so now what?" I asked David as we headed towards the main gates of the city.

David was flipping through the book filled with drawings, "The symbols are around the city. We just have to find them and follow them –"

"Find them? You make it sound as if this place is so small. This is a giant city. The largest city in the Over World. It won't be that easy."

David waved his hand at me, "The book has some drawing that give me a good idea where to start. Don't get all worked up."

"I'm not worked up."

David glanced at me and grinned, "You're a little worked up."

"Am not."

The two of us bickered to the front gate, where the guard allowed us access. We cut through the marketplace. The scent of food made my stomach grumble. I was hungry. Ignoring some people staring at me because I was a creeper, I told David I needed to eat.

"Fine, fine. Grab some food and meet me down the street, alright?" He mumbled as he took off.

I shook my head and sighed. I was worried about what David would feel when he found out this was a wild goose chase. He had been so hoping to find something amazing underneath the Sun City.

Munching on the food I had bought, I went down the street to meet up with David a few minutes later. This street was mostly empty. It had seemed to be full of shops at one point but it was as if everyone had closed it up. I knew it was silly but it felt as if we were being watched.

At the end of the street, I didn't see David. I looked around and called out for him but there was nothing. Annoyed, I walked down a side street to see if he had wandered off. I was about to call him again when I was yanked backwards.

I struggled but someone was holding me very tightly. I couldn't see them. My food fell to the ground as I tried to break free.

Then a low, strange voice in my ear said, "You and your friend need to leave. This is not a place for you."

I was released and whirled around. But whoever had grabbed me was gone. I looked up to try to see how they could have grabbed me. The wall was flat. There was no door or window they could have seen me from.

I looked down at my food, which was ruined on the dirty stone pathway, and sighed.

***

I found David a minute later. We ran into each other as I rounded the corner. I yelped in surprise.

"Geez, you okay? What took you so long?"

"Where were you?" I cried out at him, making sure he wasn't hurt.

"Sorry, I wandered away a little. I found a shop owner and was asking about this section of the city. Everything is closed here. Did you notice that?"

"That isn't important!" I said and then I told him about being grabbed and being told to leave.

David's eyes went wide and he leaned forward, "Did you see anything else?"

"No. They just told me to leave. Which we need to be doing right now. We'll stay at an inn and leave in the morning."

"Whoa, whoa, what are you talking about?"

"What are you talking about?" I asked David, "You don't mean you're going to stay."

"Of course I do. Are you kidding me? I can't leave. The fact you were warned means we are on the right track. I can't go now."

I tried not to lose my temper, "David, these people are already aware of what we are doing and all we did was walk into this section of town. We can't honestly stay. They aren't going to take that well."

"I'm staying," David replied stubbornly, "You can go if you want."

I stood there, unsure of what to do. On one hand, I wanted to go back to my village. I really did. I mean, we had been warned already by some mysterious figure. If that wasn't the biggest sign to go then I don't know what was.

But…on the other hand, this was real proof that David wasn't chasing a dream. The fact that we had been warned meant that there was some truth to this legend we were chasing. And even though I had told myself I wanted a quiet life…

"No, I'll stay."

David blinked in surprise, "You're going to stay?"

"I have to keep you out of trouble, don't I?" I said to him.

He stared at me for a second and then grinned, "Yeah, of course. Come on. You're right. Let's get some real food to eat and find an inn to stay at. We can figure out our next plan of action from there. The fact that we were warned means we should really think this through."

As we left the section of the city, I asked, "What did the store owner say when you asked him about that area?"

We were weaving our way through a crowd in a busy district of the city. The sun was starting to set. Above us, the castle shined in the setting sun. Even though it was pretty, I still couldn't stop thinking that we were probably being watched.

"He said the area is supposed to be cursed so hardly anyone opens up shop there or lives there."

"Cursed?"

"Yeah. The guy said he didn't believe in the curse though so he's had his shop there for like twenty years. He sells rare gems so people brave this apparent curse to buy from him."

"Has he seen anything weird? Like people warning him or anything?"

"No. No, he said nothing odd has happened. But it happened to us, right? I was probably talking to him at the same time you were warned…"

I frowned, "What if that guy is part of this group? He could have alerted the rest of the group to us when you went to speak to him."

"That makes sense," David admitted, "He could be part of the secret society."

We found an inn that served food. David stuffed his face but it was a little harder for me to eat. I was still distracted by that voice in the alley and what it all could mean. By the time we got to our room, David fell asleep almost instantly.

But I stayed up writing in here. Today felt really long. Somehow, so much has happened. Was that man at the shop really part of that secret society? If he was, then that entire section of town was left empty to ward people off from discovering the Moon City. The curse was just a way to scare people.

Even though I told David I was staying because I wanted to make sure he was okay…some part of me is really excited about what this could really be.

DAY 6

We set out in the early morning after breakfast. We were going to head back into the cursed section of town. We were curious to see if the man that David had spoken to yesterday was still there.

Like yesterday, the streets were empty. I was a bit jumpy. But no one came out at us and we got to the shop in good time.

"This is it but…" David stopped and together, we stared at the door.

The shop was closed. The windows had the curtains pulled over and there was a big lock on the door. David went over and knocked but there was no answer.

"Alright, so this is a bit suspicious." I said as I tried to look into one of the windows.

"Well, this pretty much confirms it, doesn't it? That he was a part of it somehow."

"Yeah, I would say so. Now what?"

"We'll just start combing this area for the symbols. The fact this group, or whatever it is, makes sure no one comes in this section of town, has to mean there is an entrance to the Moon City from here."

We left the shop and started going down the side streets, trying to find the symbol that David had seen in the book. It was strange being in such a quiet part of the Sun City. I kept straining to see if I could hear anything else, like someone coming behind us, but there was only silence.

"Hey, look at this." David said at one point.

He was crouched by an abandoned home and was pointing to something on the ground. I went over to him and was about to speak when a city guard rounded the corner.

"You two! What are you up to?"

We stood up and looked over at the guard who stared at me, "Is that a creeper?"

"Whoa, hey," David stuck his hand out, "A friendly one. Pretty sure the king told everyone about their village."

The guard narrowed his eyes at me as if I had done something wrong and asked, "What are you two doing in this area? You know it is cursed, right?"

"Cursed?" I lied, pretending that I had no idea, "We were here for the gem store. But it's closed. Is this place really cursed?"

The guard looked at me and then David before replying, "The gem store is closed?"

"That's right," David replied, "Is it normally closed?"

"No. Not that I know of anyway," He said quickly, "Now, if you two have no other business in this section, you should leave."

"Why?" I asked, still pretending I was clueless, "I mean, I know it is supposed to be cursed but there isn't any way that is really true."

The guard looked as if he didn't know what to tell us. More than likely, he had probably been told not to let anyone roam around this section of the city but was never told why he couldn't. The result was he didn't know what to do with us.

"Our inn is on the other side," David said, "We will just cut through this way."

"Well, alright. But don't hang around."

We waved good-bye and went the way we came. The guard watched us until we turned the corner and were out of sight.

"That was weird," I said, "The king definitely doesn't want people roaming around in here."

"There was one of the symbols back there, in the stone. Maybe if we walk in a circle we can get back to it and follow it."

"Maybe. Let's go this way." I said and turned around.

The person came out of nowhere. I was being pushed backwards and crashed into David. Together, we hit the ground. As we tried to get to our feet, two wither skeletons came out of a nearby abandoned building.

"Uh, this is not good." I replied as they ran over to us.

The dark figure that had knocked us down was turning around and running off.

"I can take care of the skeletons! You chase after that figure!" David yelled at me and pushed me forward.

He was right. Out of the two of us, I could run faster even if I am a creeper. Even so, I didn't like leaving him behind with the wither skeletons. I glanced at him and he told me to run.

I took off after the dark figure. It had clearly brought the wither skeletons towards us. But I wasn't going to let it go.

The figure could run quickly. Not only that but it knew the area very well. All I could do was hope to catch up with it before I lost it completely in this section. At one point, the figure jumped up and began to scale up one of the buildings.

I watched it climb and cursed. I was terrible at climbing and would be too slow. I looked down and saw a small rock. I picked it up and notched it into my bow and then let it fly.

The small rock hit the figure's leg. It was strong enough that the figure missed the next step and went falling down.

I ran over to try to catch the falling figure. I stuck out my arms and the figure slammed into me. We hit the ground and for a few seconds, I felt dizzy. But this didn't stop the person from pushing off of me and taking off at another run.

I got to my feet and chased after the mysterious person. I had thought for sure falling off a building would have stopped the figure! Whoever this was did not want to be caught.

We were reaching the outskirts of the abandoned section of the city. Was the figure really going to lead me into the city? The guards would be on me in a matter of seconds. If the mysterious individual is really a part of some secret organization, the king wouldn't stop that figure. I would be the one stopped.

The figure turned the corner and was clearly heading towards the marketplace. I had to stop the mysterious individual. Using the last of my speed, I went as fast as I could. As soon as the figure entered the marketplace, I knew that I would lose it.

I reached out and grabbed the fabric of the hoodie the figure was wearing and yanked on it. The mysterious individual was pulled backwards and fell into me. We hit the ground together but this time I wasn't going to let the figure go. I held onto the mysterious individual until it stopped struggling.

"It's over," I said, trying to catch my breath, "Don't bother trying to run again."

The figure had gone completely still. The back of the figure was against mine so I couldn't see its face. I could hear the figure gasping for air though. Somehow, even if the figure did run, I knew this mysterious person wouldn't be as fast as I was.

The figure shoved me off of it and stood up, leaning against the wall, trying to catch its breath. I got to my feet and went over to the figure. It held out its hand.

"Don't – don't come near me." The person gasped.

I reached over and pulled down the hood that was covering the face. I wasn't sure what I was expecting. A weird creature, maybe. Some sort of alien looking thing. I wasn't expecting a completely normal looking girl to be staring at me. She had large brown eyes and her hair was also brown, shoved up in a messy ponytail. She was glaring at me.

“I don’t know why you came after me,” She said, “When your friend is facing off against wither skeletons.”

“My friend is a good fighter. I’m better at running.”

“You’re a creeper,” The girl said, “What in the world are you doing?”

“You’re a human,” I snapped, “What in the world are you doing?”

She stared at me for a moment before yanking her hood back over her head, “I told you to get your friend and leave.”

“That was you in the alleyway the other day?” I asked.

She ignored me, “I’m doing this for your safety.”

“Our safety? You just sent wither skeletons after my friend.”

“Are you really that foolish? Do you not understand? What you’re trying to do – I know that you are trying to find the Moon City. I’m trying to protect you. Give up this foolish idea and go home. Go back to your village filled with the rest of the friendly creepers and live your life. Let this go.”

“First off, I am not the one who is interested in this legend. My friend is. I’m just here to try to make sure he is okay.”

“Well, you’re doing a terrible job of that. Neither one of you are okay as long as you go against the king.”

“What? Wait, didn’t he send you?”

She scowled, “No. He didn’t send me. The king – he isn’t what you think he is. Trust me, you need to –”

“Mike!”

It was David. He was nearby, calling my name. I looked over my shoulder but as soon as I did, I regretted it. The girl took off down the street. She was too fast for me to catch up to. I watched as she climbed up a side building with ease and was gone from sight.

David came around the corner and jogged up to me, "Hey! Did you hear me calling you? I took care of those skeletons. Did you catch that figure?"

"Yeah but it didn't clear anything up."

"Where is he?"

"It was a girl and she ran off when you called my name."

"A girl? She must be part of the secret society for the king."

I shook my head, "I don't think so."

I quickly told him what had happened. When I finished, David frowned as if he was trying to figure it all out.

I kept speaking, "It almost sounded as if she's part of another group trying to keep people out of the Moon City. She made it sound as if…"

"Yeah, as if the king was the bad guy here. But that's impossible, right? I've never heard anything bad had been said about the king."

"Me either. She could be lying. I don't know. What now?"

"A lot of trouble for a city we haven't even discovered yet. Come on. Let's go back to where we were and go from there."

We followed back to where we had originally gotten attacked by the wither skeletons. The street was empty. We began to backtrack to go back to where David had seen the symbol earlier in the day.

But we never made it back there. When we cut across one of the streets, an entire group of the king's guards stood there waiting for us. They even had skeletons with them.

"Halt!" One of the guards yelled.

"You're both under arrest. You were told to leave this area and have refused. We need to bring you to the dungeon." The guard we had seen earlier said to us.

"What?" I blurted out, "To the dungeon? Doesn't that seem a little excessive?"

"You have been warned and ignored the warning. You can come quietly or we can make things difficult for you."

David shook his head at me, "Don't try to fight them. We can't take on that many guards."

"So, we're just going to get tossed into a dungeon?"

The guards came over to us. We stayed still as they yanked us towards the castle, towards the dungeons.

I knew this was all wrong. We technically hadn't broken any laws. Was what that girl had been saying correct? Was the king not as good as we had thought he was?

We were brought to the castle but not through the main entrance. Instead, we were pulled in through the side and taken down three levels to the dungeon far below the castle. This was where the worst criminals were housed. Not people who walked into a section of town that they were asked to leave before.

This was all wrong. I had been denying it before but David had to be right – there had to be something big enough to hide that two people walking around the city would be shoved into the dungeon.

We were tossed into a cell and the door was locked behind us. There was a torch offering light to see by. We had a barred window on the door but all it showed were other cells.

They had taken our weapons but my journal had been tucked close to me and they hadn't found it. That was comforting, at least.

When we were alone, I said to David, "Uh, okay, can you explain why we didn't fight those guys? Now we are stuck in this dungeon."

"We didn't fight because they would have just gotten rid of us for good. At least down here, we have a chance at escaping." David said as he ran his hands over the walls, as if there was going to be some sort of secret entrance.

I was trying not to panic. There was something scary about being under the castle in this prison. No one would know we were down here. There would be no one coming to rescue us.

"Man, we should have listened to that girl." I complained.

"Too late now."

I sat down on the ground and pulled out my journal. By the torchlight, I was able to catch up in here. It took a lot to write this all down but like before, I want to have a record of things.

I'm just trying not to think about being stuck down here for ages.

DAY 7

"I don't think this is food." David said, pointing to the slop at the plate that we had been given for dinner.

The guard only grunted and walked off. I looked down at my own plate and wrinkled my nose. It looked disgusting. I didn't even want to think about what it was.

"David, I think we are in over our heads."

He chuckled, "What gave that away?"

"I will admit that I think there has to be some truth now to the Moon City. I mean, we've been warned by some mysterious girl and then the king just throws us into the dungeons with virtually no reason."

"Right. So we know that section of the town isn't cursed. It has to be the entrance to the city. And there are two groups involved. The secret society with the king and whatever group that girl is a part of."

"While it is great that we have this information, what exactly are we going to do with it? We are stuck down here."

"I don't know. Get some sleep, I guess. Maybe something will come to us if we get some rest."

It was a poor plan but it wasn't as if we had any other ideas. I curled up on the thin bed in the corner as David got into the other one. But it felt almost impossible to fall asleep. Even though we had faced down scary things before, I was still worried we would be stuck down here forever.

Even with my panic, I must have fallen asleep because I woke up later to a soft noise outside our door. Alarmed, I sat up. David was snoring. How could he be so fast asleep that he was snoring? He amazed me sometimes.

Then I heard the noise again. It was like a soft scraping noise. With my heart pounding, I slipped out of the bed and went over to the door. I tried to look through the barred window and see who it was.

"Whose there?" I whispered in the darkness.

"Be quiet." Came a voice that sounded oddly familiar.

I looked down and could just make out a hooded figure messing around with the lock on our cell. My eyes widened as I realized who it was.

"Hey, it's you."

"Do you not understand what being quiet means?" She snapped.

It was the girl that I had chased in the alley. She was still wearing her hood but I could see her eyes glance up at me as she fiddled with the lock. I decided to listen to her. If she wanted to break us out, I wasn't going to complain.

There was a tiny clicking noise as the lock turned and then the door opened. She pointed to David and gestured for me to wake him up. I went over to him and shook him awake.

"Wh-what?" He mumbled.

"We have to go. Now. Be quiet and come on."

David's eyes grew wide when he saw the girl in the doorway. I could tell he wanted to ask questions but knew better because we had to be quiet. He got his feet and we followed the girl.

The hallway was dark. I was worried someone would see us but it was as if there were no guards at all. I thought we were going to go up the stairs but the girl yanked us towards the opposite direction – further into the dungeon.

"Uh-" David spoke up but the girl raised her hand, silencing him.

We followed her down the hallway. I was worried other people in the cells would hear us but there was nothing. I wondered if maybe I was dreaming. But I pinched myself and felt a stab of pain and knew we were all really doing this.

When we got to the end of the hallway, there was nowhere else to go. I looked at the girl, waiting for her to realize that there had been some sort of mistake. But she crouched down and pressed her hand against the floor.

There was a dull light from her hands and then the floor vanished to show a tunnel underneath. I heard David gasp behind me. Had she just done magic? I had never seen something like that before.

She jumped down into the tunnel and motioned for us to follow. David pushed past me, suddenly eager to get closer to the girl and her magic. He hopped down into the tunnel. I looked behind me. Sure, we were leaving – but with who, exactly?

I jumped down into the tunnel. The girl raised her hand upwards and the stones reappeared, blocking us from the dungeon. Everything was pitch dark. For a few seconds, all I could hear were the three of us breathing.

Then the girl snapped her fingers and a small flame illuminated the tunnel. It was coming from her fingertips.

"Okay, what is this?" I asked her, "Magic?"

"You're part of the Moon City, aren't you? I mean, you live there." David said excitedly.

"What?" I asked him, "She lives in the Moon City?"

"I read it in the book. I read how people lived in the Moon City and one day they all vanished. It was as if they just got sucked up into thin air. But they had magical powers. They were born in The End and moved into the Moon City. You're descended from them, aren't you?" David sounded so excited as if he had just been given a diamond sword.

"Yes," The girl said after a long pause, "I am from the Moon City."

"What's your name? I'm David. This is Mike. Why did you save us? Where are we going?"

"My name is Star," The girl answered, "And I saved you because you're both too foolish to listen to me. I told you to leave. The king doesn't care who you are. He wants the Moon City for himself. He doesn't want anyone trying to find it. As for where we are going, I'm escorting you outside of the city. Go home."

She pushed past us but David scuttled after her, "What? We can't go home. Mike, tell her we can't go home."

"I wouldn't mind going home, actually."

David ignored me, "We want to see the Moon City. You know how to follow the symbols and get in there, don't you?"

"I know how to get to my home, if that is what you are asking me." Star replied in a frosty tone.

"I've been reading about the Moon City for so long! I knew the king was probably part of some secret group –"

Star spun around, "The king – every king since the war – has wanted to keep the Moon City for himself. My people have to hide because if the king finds us, he will get rid of us. All of our treasure, our money, our knowledge the kings over the years have stolen for themselves. This current king included. They don't want anyone to know about the Moon City because they are greedy. The king will not allow you to just waltz into our city. Neither will I. I saved you because you are both silly individuals looking for adventure. But you have to go home now."

She stared at the two of us, waiting for one of us to speak. I didn't know what to say. Everything she had said was true. We were probably over our heads. The Moon City was clearly protected by the king. If there really were people who still lived in the Moon City, there was no way they would want us creeping around.

But I knew David wasn't going to just let this go. This was something he wanted to discover. I braced myself for the fight that was going to rage between him and Star.

"Why not expose the king? Come out of hiding and show everyone the Moon City?" He asked her.

Star set off walking again and we followed her. She was quiet and I wondered if she was just going to ignore what David had asked.

But then she said, "We can't do that."

"Well, why not?" He pressed.

But Star shook her head, "We just can't. You don't need to know why."

"If the king is doing this, people need to know. They need to know he isn't some great guy. Whatever you guys have in the city, we can figure it out."

"You two are going home tonight. That's the end of this discussion."

David glanced at me but didn't say anything. No matter what Star said, I somehow knew that it wasn't going to be the end of the discussion. David wanted into that city.

We walked in the tunnel for what felt like thirty minutes. When we got to the end of the tunnel, Star pushed open a grate and crawled out. We followed after her and ended up in a small empty house. It was covered in dust and there were a few candles lighting the room up.

"What is this?"

"An abandoned house. But we use it to get to the tunnels below the city."

"Is this the entrance to the Moon City?" David asked her.

"I wouldn't be stupid enough to bring you to the entrance of the city." She said to us.

She handed up two bags. They had some food shoved in them for our trip back home.

"Thanks." I said to her.

Star nodded and went, "You have to leave tonight. The king will know we set you free. It isn't safe to stay."

"What about you?" I asked her.

"I'll go back home for a little bit, let the others know you are gone."

"And then what? You guys just keep hiding?" David asked her, "Is that all you guys do? You are descendants from this great city and all you do is hide from the king?"

"David, don't," I said to him, "My people hid too."

"Yeah but when the Nether portals started opening up in your village, your people went out and found help. Your people need help too."

Star narrowed her eyes at him, "My people don't need help. We have lived this way for thousands of years, constantly in battle with the king. We are protecting things you couldn't ever understand."

David opened his mouth to fight with her some more but he didn't get a chance to. Just then, the front door of the abandoned house we were hiding in was kicked down. In came a group of skeletons, all holding swords and shields.

"Looks like we've been discovered." David said as he looked around for a weapon of his own.

"Drat. Listen, I'll hold them off but you two need to go!" Star shouted over her shoulder as she took a step forward.

"What? You can't fend them off!"

The first skeleton lunged and Star snapped her fingers. The flame that she had in the palm of her hand seemingly exploded into a fireball. It crashed into the skeleton and sent it flying back. It crumbled into ash.

"Okay, maybe she can." David said and then we were running out the back exit.

Behind us, we could hear the fireballs exploding against the skeletons. We pushed out of the back door and spilled out into the city streets. But skeletons were here waiting for us as well. Alarmed, I ducked just as one tried to swing it's sword at me. I reached up and grab its bony hand and yanked the sword out of its hand.

Then I brought the sword down on the skeleton. Next to me, David had managed to disarm another skeleton and take its sword as well. We began to cut through the skeletons that had been sent to take us back to the dungeon.

There were a ton of them. It was a crazy amount that had been sent this way, as if the king was determined to toss us back into the dungeon no matter what. As we got pinned against the wall of a house, Star appeared. She had lighting glowing out of her fingertips. Her skin had turned a strange shade of blue. I had never, ever seen something like that before.

She raised her hands and the lightning hit all the skeletons. They turned to ash almost right away. All we could do was stare in amazement.

"Uh, wow. Okay. So. Back to the magic thing," David said, "Want to expand on that a bit?"

But Star had gone very pale. She took a step forward and looked as if she was going to fall over. I reached out and grabbed her before she could fall.

"Too much powers used tonight. I'm weak." She managed to say.

"Not good. This is not good." I mumbled, making sure I had a firm grip on her.

"Star, listen to me. More are going to come. But we aren't leaving the city. So where can we go?" David asked her.

"Maybe we should go." I said to him.

"What, why?"

"Are you serious, David? Star said this is how her people live. This isn't up for us to intrude on. If they're hiding something from the king, then we can't just expect for them to let them into their city. We already have guards coming after us. We were thrown into a dungeon. Star used too much magic. You have to ask yourself if you are being selfish because you want to see the city or if you really care about Star's people."

I could see David wrestling with what to do. We could hear more skeletons coming down towards us.

Finally, he said, "You're right. But we can't just leave Star here. She's passed out because of us. Come on."

I picked Star up, who was limp in our arms. Holding her, we took off at a run away from the skeleton noises. We weren't sure where we could go but we knew we had to lose the guards somehow.

"This was such a terrible idea." I said to David.

"Exciting though, right?" He said as we rounded a corner.

We cut across the market place which was empty since it was the middle of the night. Star's skin was still pale. I hoped that she would be okay. I didn't know anything about magic use but she had still used a lot of it to protect us. We had to make sure she was okay too.

"I really regret coming along." I said in between gasping for air as we ran.

"Ah, come on. Lucas the creeper king was way worse than this."

"That's like saying being trapped with a bunch of ghasts is better than being trapped with a bunch of zombie pig men. Neither one is fun." I exclaimed.

David only grinned at me. What else could he say? Maybe he just loved this sort of adventure.

We passed by a fountain and a couple of bakeries. We had no idea where we needed to go. The skeletons didn't seem to be easing up on us. As we turned another corner, we came to a complete stop.

In front of us was none other than the king.

He looked at us and then to Star and a cold smile crossed his face, "Found you."

ABOUT THE AUTHOR

Mark Mulle is a passionate Minecraft gamer who writes game guides, short stories, and novels about the Minecraft universe. He has been exploring, building, and fighting in the game ever since its launch, and he often uses in-game experiences for inspiration on creating the best fiction for fellow fans of the game. He works as a professional writer and splits his time between gaming, reading, and storytelling, three hobbies and lifelong passions that he attributes to a love of roleplaying, a pursuit of challenging new perspectives, and a visceral enjoyment the vast worlds that imagination has to offer. His favorite thing to do, after a long day of creating worlds both on and off the online gaming community, is to relax with his dog, Herobrine, and to unwind with a good book. His favorite authors include Stephen King, Richard A. Knaak, George R. R. Martin, and R. A. Salvatore, whose fantasy works he grew up reading or is currently reading. Just like in Minecraft, Mark always strives to level up, so to speak, so that he can improve his skills and continue to surprise his audience. He prefers to play massive multiplayer online games but often spends time in those games fighting monsters one on one and going solo against the toughest mobs and bosses he can manage to topple. In every game, his signature character build is a male who focuses mostly on crafting weapons and enchanting, and in every battle, he always brings a one hander sword and a shield with as much magical attributes as he can pour into them. Because he always plays alone, he likes to use his game guides to share all the secrets and knowledge he gains, and who know—he may have snuck some information into his fiction as well. Keep an eye out for his next book!

Disclaimer
This is a work of fiction. Names, characters, businesses, places, events and incidents are either the products of the author's imagination or used in fictitious manner. Any resemblance to actual persons, living or dead, or actual events is purely coincidental.

Author's Note: This short story is for your reading pleasure. The characters in this "Minecraft Adventure Series" such as Steve, Endermen or Herobrine...etc. are based on the Minecraft Game coming from Minecraft ®/TM & © 2009-2013 Mojang / Notch

CPSIA information can be obtained
at www.ICGtesting.com
Printed in the USA
LVOW13s1954220217
525093LV00010B/1120/P